REALM OF RAMION

To Alasdair
with love from Granny.   Christmas 2005.

Collected stories:

Ramion
Realm of Ramion

Individual stories:

The Land of Lost Hair
The Vicar's Chickens
The Crystal Key
Creatures of the Forest

The Dim Daft Dwarves
The Bands of Evil
The Magic Magpie
The Cruel Count

REALM OF RAMION

Frank Hinks

Perronet

Published by
Perronet Press
The Old Vicarage,
Shoreham,
Sevenoaks,
Kent TN14 7SB
www.frankhinks.com

A CIP record for this book is available from the British Library

ISBN 09543733-5-9

Printed in Times New Roman by Richard Edward Limited
Plumstead SE28 0AB

For

Julius, Alexander

and Benjamin

My special thanks to

Katie kingshill for editing

the text and my wife

without whose encouragement

and criticism the

illustrations would not exist.

CONTENTS

The Dim Daft Dwarves

The Bands of Evil

The Magic Magpie

The Cruel Count

THE

DIM DAFT DWARVES

I

Griselda looked into her crystal ball and cried out to her pet skull: "Boris come here! Look at the boys playing in the garden of The Old Vicarage, so juicy, so very good to eat. Guards! Bring me the magic cauldron."

The dwarves brought the magic cauldron to Griselda. "Now I need just a pinch of stardust. Julioso, go and get it."

Julioso climbed up a ladder, got the box of stardust from the top of the cupboard and came running to Griselda. Aliano and Benjio were playing on the ground with the snakes and spiders. Julioso tripped over Aliano's outstretched foot sending the box of stardust spinning through the air. It landed in the magic cauldron and there was a great explosion. Griselda disappeared.

When the dwarves saw what they had done they trembled with fear. They huddled in a heap upon the ground waiting for Griselda to return, to scream, shout, rant, rage and reduce their height to two foot three. But nothing happened. They spent days huddled together not knowing what to do, for they had never done a thing without being shouted at or kicked.

After a week they suddenly became brave, got up, looked around and whispered, "She's gone for ever!" They began to dance and sing, "Who's afraid of the big bad witch? The big bad witch! The big bad witch!" Until the wind rustled in the trees and, afraid that Griselda had returned, they ran and hid.

After a month Julioso had an idea (a rare occurrence).

"Let's go fishing," he said.

"We don't know how."

"Let's give it a try."

So the dwarves found sticks, hooks and string and went down to the river bank. They did not have a lot of luck. They caught three boots, three cans and a mouldy vest. Then their hooks got stuck in a tractor tyre deep in the river bed. They thought that they had caught a fish (the biggest fish in the world) tried to pull it to the river bank and with a splash all fell in.

"Dim daft dwarves," sighed Boris. "I had better show them how to fish." The skull floated down. "You need some bait. Wriggling worms are best."

The dwarves looked at Boris in amazement: they had never thought of that. They returned to the river bank where Boris showed them how to cast the line and land the fish. They spent a happy afternoon casting their lines and falling in.

"Three trout. One pike. Not bad," hissed Boris with a toothy grin, as Aliano fell in for the seventh time and a pike bit him on the bottom. "Let's go home and cook supper."

They returned to the glade deep within the forest where Boris showed the dwarves how to cook the fish in a white wine sauce with just a touch of garlic.

The dwarves had never eaten anything so nice. "Wonderful!" "Great!" "Brilliant!" they enthused, licking their lips. "Better than dragon's blood." "Or mashed newt." "Or rhino sick."

The next day Aliano had an idea (a rare occurrence). "Let's do some gardening," he said. "I'm fed up with nettles and brambles. Let's have some flowers." So off they went to the garden centre, bought lots and lots of packets of seed, and took them back to the glade deep within the forest.

"What do we do now?" asked Julioso and Benjio. Aliano pretended that he knew. "We dig a hole, put a packet in the hole and in a little while flowers pop up."

They dug a hole, put in a packet and stood back waiting for flowers to pop up. But nothing happened. "That's odd." "Odd." "Very odd indeed."

"I can't stand much more of this," groaned Boris, banging himself against a tree. "I had better show those silly dwarves how to plant the seed."

"You dim daft dwarves have no more brains than a pickled newt. You take the seed out of the packet. Then cover the seed with soil." The dwarves looked at Boris in amazement: they had never thought of that. "First you chase away the snakes and spiders. Then you clear the weeds. Then you dig the soil. Then you sow the seed. In a few months (if you weed and water) flowers will appear."

The dwarves were disappointed and gathered in a huddle talking excitedly: "They don't just pop up?" "Out of the packet?" "Cover the seed with soil?" "Fancy that!" "Sounds like hard work!" "Let's give it a try." "All right."

The dwarves found some carpet beaters and, standing in a line, walked through the glade beating the ground (and sometimes by mistake each other) shouting: "Scram!" "Vamoosh!" "Get out of it!" until the snakes and spiders packed their bags and crept away.

Armed with shears, slashers and machetes, the dwarves sheared and slashed nettles, brambles and thickets and burnt the lot in a bonfire, which Boris lit with laser beams from his sockets where once were eyes. Then with fork and spade they dug the ground, moaning and groaning: "This is hard work. To think we thought you put a packet in the ground and then the flowers popped up."

Boris ordered a lorry load of manure. The driver leant out of the cab and shouted: "Where do you want it?" Boris floated down to tell him, but when the driver saw a skull floating through the air with blazing red sockets instead of eyes he panicked. He pressed the tipper switch (tipping the manure over Aliano) and drove away at high speed. Julioso and Benjio put clothes pegs on their noses and dug poor Aliano out. He stank.

"You had better go fishing!" shouted Boris from the top of a tree. He knew that Aliano was bound to fall in.

The dwarves planted the seed, watered and hoed the weeds, then knelt down in the mud, putting ears to the earth trying to hear the growing seed. "Can't hear a thing." "Nothing's happening." "Dim daft dwarves," said Boris from the tree as, with a yawn, he fell asleep.

After a few weeks tiny green shoots began to push out of the earth. "They're growing," shouted Julioso excitedly, pouring the watering can over the head of Aliano who was bending down looking at the tiny shoots. "Hip, hip, hooray!" shouted Aliano, jumping to his feet and stuffing a hose pipe down Benjio's trousers. "Great! Great! Great!" shouted Benjio, turning on the sprinkler.

The dwarves held hands, danced in the spray, sang of flowers and summer sun. They sang of the joy of living without Griselda.

II

Whenever stardust gets a chance to wrap itself around a witch, it binds her tight and sends her whizzing through the void to the Land of Krall. That is what happened to Griselda. When the box of stardust landed in the magic cauldron, the explosion sent stardust all over Griselda. It wrapped itself around her, bound her tight and with a strange whistling sound sent her whizzing through the void. She would have screamed but her dress swirled up (revealing a pair of ancient bloomers) and stuffed itself inside her mouth.

She landed in a muddy bog which sucked her down and down, her feet disappearing, then her calves. "Help! Help!" she cried. The words echoed through the distant night, but there came no help. Her knees disappeared, then her thighs.

"Those damned dwarves!" Griselda cursed, in her fury reaching up and grasping the branch of a dead tree which stood gaunt beside the bog.

"Damn those dwarves!" she cursed again. Her fury gave her strength and she pulled upon the branch, screamed and pulled again. Slowly her thighs and calves emerged from the bog. With a burp her feet shot from the clinging mud, leaving her bedraggled body dangling from the branch.

"Those damned dwarves!" Griselda gasped, as she pulled her body up into the tree, climbed along the branch and fell exhausted to solid earth.

The Land of Krall is a place of shadows ruled by the night. There are three moons. No sun ever shines. Volcanoes belch liquid fire into the night sky. Mud oozes. Beasts howl and curse the night.

For a witch brought up in the south of England it was a shock. Griselda was not pleased at all. "When I get home I shall chop those dim daft dwarves into little bits and feed them to the crows." Griselda would have said more but at that moment three witches rushed past screaming, "Run! Run! The giants come!"

It was the annual witch hunt. Giants (toymakers from the neighbouring planet of Aaron) had come to replenish their stock of witches for their children's toys. Against the sky were huge figures, carrying nets and jars and sounding hunting horns.

Griselda tried to run but was too slow. A net swished down and scooped her up. "Got one!" grunted the giant as he placed a huge clammy hand in the net and picked Griselda up between finger and thumb. She screamed and cursed. "She's really ugly! The children will love her!" the giant enthused as he dropped Griselda in a storage jar and sealed the lid.

"They will not!" Griselda shrieked as she hammered on the jar. She tried to remember the spell for turning giants into newts but failed. The giant laughed and lifting the lid dropped in a capsule of sleeping gas. Griselda fell asleep.

III

Not long after the seed began to grow Benjio had an idea (a very rare occurrence). "Let's do some decorating," he said.

Griselda lived in a ruined tower, all that remained of Grunch Castle. There were holes in the roof, walls covered in green slime. Damp rose from the dungeon to the vaulted hall where Griselda had her throne of slimy stone. In her bedroom on the floor above, plaster crumbled off the walls, slime oozed. The dwarves lived in a shed propped up against the tower wall.

"It would be nice to live inside the tower," murmured Julioso. "Mrs G. has gone for ever," said Benjio, who was extremely dim and never got things right. "Let's live inside the tower."

So off the dwarves went to the shop, bought pots of paint and took them back to the glade deep within the forest. They opened a pot and were just about to paint a slimy green wall when Boris awoke and saw what they were doing. "No! No! No! You cannot paint a wall of oozing green slime. You need to mend the roof, cure the rising damp, clean off the slime, replace the perished plaster, cover with lining paper and then you paint."

The dwarves gathered in a huddle. "Sounds an awful lot of work." "But it would be nice not to live in a shed." "To be warm and dry." "And live in style." "Let's give it a try." "All right."

Boris showed the dwarves how to rig a pulley to lift new timbers to the top of the tower. Julioso and Aliano pulled on the rope. The timbers were very heavy. Slowly they rose from the ground. Benjio was on the top of the tower to take the timbers when they reached him.

Julioso and Aliano pulled harder and harder. The timbers had nearly reached the top, when Julioso's bottom began to itch and he let go to give it a scratch. Two dwarves were heavier than the timbers but not one. The timbers began to fall. As the timbers (on one end of the rope) came down Aliano (on the other end) shot up. "Let go," bellowed Boris.

Aliano's brain was very slow. Just before he reached the top of the tower he let go. By then he was travelling so fast that he whistled through the air past the ear of Benjio, who tried to catch him, missed and with a scream fell off the tower. Julioso (who had finished scratching his bottom) was wandering round in circles wondering where Aliano had gone. The timbers landed on his toe: he hopped and yelled in pain, but did not look up. Benjio landed on his head. They fell in a heap upon the ground. Meanwhile Aliano had shot over the tower, and disappeared into the forest.

After five or ten minutes Julioso and Benjio sorted out their tangled limbs (fortunately dwarves are fairly tough). "We must find Aliano!" Benjio cried. "We must mount an exhibition."

Julioso did not think that this was the time for art. "How about an expedition?" With ruck sacks on their backs and trousers done up with bicycle clips, the dwarves set off with Boris and found Aliano suspended by his braces up the highest tree. Boris floated up and tied a rope to a branch beside his head.

Aliano was afraid of heights. He was too scared to undo his braces and climb down the rope. He would not move. Boris was tired of dim daft dwarves. Getting out his gnashers, he gave Aliano a sharp nip upon the bottom. "Help! Help! Boris! No!" screamed Aliano, as he scrambled down the tree with Boris gnashing at his bottom.

"You lot are hopeless," Boris groaned. "My cousin Bert is a builder. He can come and do the work." Bert had a shock when Boris telephoned. "But I thought you lost your head." "No, no," said Boris. "I lost my body. I've still got my head."

Boris used Griselda's gold to persuade Bert to come and do the work. Bert did not enjoy working in a glade deep within a forest with three dwarves and a floating skull, even if the skull was his cousin Boris, but he mended the roof, stopped the rising damp, and replastered the walls.

The dwarves tried to help. There were times when a dwarf managed to get a piece of wallpaper on a wall but as soon as he turned his back the wallpaper sprang off, curled itself around him and pinned him to the ground. The dwarves were unable to climb a ladder without falling off and though they got a little paint on the ceilings and the wood, most flowed over the floor or on to themselves.

By the time Bert finished, the tower was extremely smart. Wood and ceilings were painted. The walls were papered in a dainty design with matching curtains and blinds. The dwarves even scraped the ooze and slime off Griselda's throne until the white stone shone as new. They did not like the little devils on the corners of the throne, so they put on a fitted cover to match the curtains and blinds.

The dwarves cleaned and polished, put pot plants on the dresser. They even installed a gas fire with artificial logs. "But there is not a gas pipe within five miles!" groaned Boris, banging his skull against the wall.

By the time the work was finished it was late summer. The tower was surrounded by a garden: green lawns, and long rows of bright yellow sunflowers.

IV

When Griselda awoke she found herself strapped to a chair in a black windowless room. She could not see a thing. Suddenly the room began to move up and down, round and round and up and down again, leaving Griselda dangling upside down from the chair. There was the sound of ripping paper and excited cries of, "Thanks Mum!" "Thanks Dad!" "A witch-in-a-box!" "Just what we wanted!"

The box was turned right way up and with a bump placed on a table. Large childish fingers fumbled for the catch and Griselda hurtled upwards. The chair was on the end of a huge metal spring. Griselda screamed and cursed as large clammy hands pushed her down back into the box, fingers fumbled for the catch and once again she hurtled upwards.

"Mum! Mum! Isn't she cross!" cried the giant children, pointing at Griselda.

Griselda was cross. She was very cross indeed. When Griselda is cross she is very dangerous. Summoning all her magic powers she sent thunderbolts to get the children. The children laughed and laughed as the thunderbolts bounced backwards and forwards all around Griselda. "Great magic, Mum!" "Thanks, Dad!"

The giant toymakers had placed a protective force field all around Griselda. The instructions read : "Thanks to the anti-magic force field your children can play in complete safety. See the magic spin and turn. No matter how cross the witch gets, her magic cannot reach them."

But the makers had reckoned without Griselda. As she shot once more out of the box she directed all her magic powers down towards the chair on which she was sitting.

The chair sprang loose from the metal coil and Griselda flew through the protective force field. As she passed out of it, magic crackled from her fingers, spiders crawled down the necks of the children, snakes wound themselves around them and ants scurried in their pants. The children screamed and screamed. Their parents turned white in horror.

"That's the last time we buy toys from the Bargain Toy Store." "Send it back to the maker." "Let loose the mice." "They'll get her!"

Griselda hurtled upwards, whizzed out of a window and landed deep inside a forest. "Curse those dim daft dwarves!" she cried. "When I get home I'll eat them for my supper."

Griselda would have said more but at that moment she heard the whir of vast metal clockwork mice let loose to get her. With a scream she scrambled to her feet and ran.

V

"Mrs G. has gone for ever." "We must celebrate." "I wonder how." The dwarves needed an idea and stood around for days scratching their heads, until Boris hissed: "How about a feast?" "Great idea!" "Why didn't we think of that?" "I'm sure that we would have. In about a week."

It was such a special occasion that each dwarf had a bath (they did this once a year), changed his underclothes (they did this twice a year) and went into town for a haircut (instead of using the garden shears). Boris could hardly believe his eyes (or nose) when he saw (and smelt) the dwarves so clean and smart. The dwarves then took some of Griselda's gold and went into town to buy some new clothes. They came back wearing the latest surfing gear and carrying surf boards under their arms. "But there isn't a surfing beach within a hundred miles!" groaned Boris, banging himself against a tree.

All the preparations for the feast went well. Nothing was spilt or burnt. Before they sat down to eat Boris passed round glasses of champagne, balancing the tray upon his head. The dwarves clinked glasses: "Good health," "Cheers," "Bottoms up." But in their hearts they suddenly felt fear.

The dwarves served the first course. As they began to eat, it began to rain outside. The wind howled. The sky grew dark though it was mid-day. They felt a sense of doom.

No one was hungry. As Julioso rose to propose the toast "To absent friends," the tower shook as thunder and lightning crashed and flashed and split the sky. The oak doors burst open: in walked Griselda. "But I am absent no longer, Julioso," she hissed.

The three dwarves hid beneath the table. Boris floated up to the rafters and pretended to be asleep. Griselda raised her magic staff and sent a thunderflash which echoed in his bony skull. "Come here!" she shrieked. Boris floated down. "Guards get out from beneath the table." Three heads appeared. They scrambled out and knelt before Griselda, shaking with fear.

Griselda was in a filthy temper. "That stardust sent me to the Land of Krall. It has taken months to travel back. What are those yellow things in a row beside the fattening cages?" "Sunflowers." "What are they doing there?" "We thought the place needed brightening up." "Brightening up! I'll brighten up your bottoms!" Griselda hissed as she lifted her foot and gave each dwarf a kick.

Griselda raised her magic staff and sent out a thunderflash: sunflowers withered and died, nettles and brambles sprang up, snakes and spiders came scurrying back. She looked at the dwarves in disgust: "You're clean! You're smart! I can see that you have been trying to be good." "Oh no, mistress! We've been bad." "Bad." "Very bad." "Shut up."

Griselda raised her magic staff. The dwarves' hair grew wild. Then she saw the dainty wallpaper. "How twee! How nice! How ..." she spluttered in disgust. She raised her magic staff: the wallpaper curled up and burnt, holes appeared in the roof, damp rose from the dungeon, slime oozed out of the walls, curtains, blinds and the fitted cover burst into flame.

"Where did you get the money for the building work?" demanded Griselda.

The dwarves did not say a thing. Boris mumbled about a gift from his Great-Aunt Edith. Griselda leered at him. "I can always tell a lie. I love a lie. You used my gold didn't you?" Boris stuttered, "Yes," fearfully waiting for the thunderflash to echo in his bony skull. But nothing happened.

"Ah Boris, Boris, my dear," murmured Griselda, suddenly in a better mood. "Come to Griselda. I shall scratch your bony head. There is nothing like a little theft. I am glad you have not become good like these disgusting dwarves." She turned to the food, dipped a finger in a dish and made a horrid face. "What, no dragon's blood! No mashed newt! No rhino sick! Go and buy some."

The dwarves ran out into the rain. "Rhino sick! Ugh!" they cried as they dashed off to get Griselda's shopping.

THE

BANDS OF EVIL

I

As Scrooey-Looey walked through the farmer's field he was approached by a horrid hag carrying a tray of bubble-mixture around her neck. Each bottle was labelled "Super whizzo bubble-mixture. The biggest bubbles in the world." "Good morning, Mr Scrooey-Looey," said the horrid hag politely.

"Morning, hag," replied the rabbit. "My goodness! You are in need of plastic surgery."

The horrid hag trembled with anger but ignoring the remark continued politely: "Would you like to buy some boys a present? The best bubble-mixture in the world. Three bottles for 1p."

Scrooey-Looey had never bought anyone a present but three bottles for 1p was a bargain. Without thinking he handed over 1p, grabbed the bottles and ran, muttering to himself, "I've really got a bargain!" As he ran back to The Old Vicarage, the horrid hag laughed and disappeared.

Scrooey-Looey found the boys in the garden. They ran to him. "Bubble-mixture!" "Thank you, Scrooey-Looey," they cried, as they unscrewed the lids, dipped in the sticks and blew huge bubbles. The bubbles went right over them and trapped inside they floated up into the sky.

Scrooey-Looey was so shocked at what he had done that without thinking he climbed the highest tree (though he was scared of heights) and jumped off on to the bubble containing Benjamin as it soared up from below. He hung on and shut his eyes. The bubbles floated above the trees. A strange wind blew and carried them away towards the ruined tower in the glade deep within the forest.

Boris the skull was floating above the tower, looking out towards the village. "I can see three bubbles. One has a furry thing on top." "A furry thing!" exclaimed Griselda. "What is it?"

"A rabbit!" hissed Boris. "It must be Scrooey-Looey." "I'm not eating him," murmured Griselda. "He's so rude and disagreeable he would give me belly-ache. I shall use him to make a pair of white gloves. The carrion crow can eat the rest."

Inside the bubbles the boys could see the ruined tower. Scrooey-Looey still had his eyes shut tight as the bubbles landed lightly on the ground at Griselda's feet. "Run, Scrooey-Looey," shouted Benjamin. The rabbit jumped and ran.

"Catch him, guards," commanded Griselda. But the dwarves were too slow. They tripped over each other's feet and landed in a heap. Scrooey-Looey disappeared into the forest and hid in the bushes.

Griselda raised her magic staff and burst the bubbles. The boys fell to the earth amidst slimy, disgusting bubble-mixture. "Seize them, guards. Put them in the fattening cages."

The boys kicked and fought but, after a struggle, the dwarves threw them in the cages. "Ah, that is better," said Griselda poking Benjamin with her magic staff through the bars of the cage. "They are very bony. They need fattening up. Get the fattening mixture."

The dwarves went to the cages. They were too strong for the boys, and though the boys put up a fight, it was not long before they were fed. The dwarves hobbled away moaning loudly "Spat the mixture up my nose", "Kicked my shin," "Bit my ear".

Griselda looked in her cookery book. "Now let me see. I took a recipe from the Daily Witch and popped it in here. Ah, here it is. Pot roast for boys. I shall need dragon's blood, mashed newt, wings of bat and wriggling worms. I don't suppose you've got them," she cried looking at the dwarves. "Got the lot." "Good. The boys have fattened nicely. Throw them in the pot."

"Oh no," murmured Scrooey-Looey from behind the bushes. "How can I save them?" He could think of nothing.

II

Julioso took Julius, Aliano Alexander, Benjio Benjamin. The boys were so fat they could not struggle. The dwarves swung the boys in the air. Then the dwarves did a strange thing. They never knew themselves whether it was because that morning they were especially dim or because deep down they wanted to save the boys. But when they swung the boys in the air they flung them in the magic cauldron not the cooking pot. With loud cries the boys disappeared.

When Griselda saw what the dwarves had done, she screamed and screamed and screamed. The noise was so great Boris floated to the top of the highest tree. The dwarves ran and hid. "Do not think that you can hide from me," bellowed Griselda. She raised her magic staff: Julioso shot out from behind a water tower which stood to one side of the ruined tower and landed at her feet. She raised her magic staff again: Aliano flew out of a window of an attic in the ruined tower and landed on top of Julioso. She raised her magic staff the third time: Benjio shot out of a pile of manure and landed on top of Julioso and Aliano.

The dwarves trembled before Griselda. She raised her magic staff, uttered an ancient spell and bands of crystal appeared around their necks and wrists; at the front of each band there was a grinning skull.

"Go to Ramion and recapture my supper. When you find a boy take a band off your wrist and put it round his neck. The band will expand to any size. Rub the skull at the front and then the boy will travel to me. Once you have returned the boys to my tender care, rub the skull at the front of the band around your necks and you will also return to me. Do not fail to recapture the boys and then return or I shall come and atomise your cringing bodies."

Atomise was too hard a word for the dwarves to understand, but they knew it could not be nice to be atomised. "No, mistress," they stammered as they felt the hard bands around their necks. "We will not fail." "Now go." So saying, Griselda kicked the dwarves into the magic cauldron: with cries they disappeared. Griselda went into the tower. As soon as she had gone Scrooey-Looey crept out from behind the bushes, jumped into the magic cauldron and disappeared.

The boys landed deep within a jungle. They had returned to their normal size and picking themselves up walked slowly between the trees. They were tired and did not know that Griselda's guards were only just behind.

They saw flowers in the shape of trumpets, bent down and picked them. Soon their arms were full of flowers. A gentle breeze blew and the trumpets began to play a merry tune. The boys danced and danced until exhausted they lay down on a bank beside a jungle stream and fell asleep, flowers strewn all around.

The dwarves landed deep within the jungle, one on top of another. It took a long time to untangle muddled arms and legs. At last they got up, looked around and found a print from Benjamin's shoe. "The boys have been here. We must track them down."

When Scrooey-Looey landed, he gave a scream of delight: he was in a forest of lettuces and carrots fifty foot high. "Great! Great! Great! More! More! More!" he shouted as he began to eat.

Scrooey-Looey forgot all about the boys and the need to warn them that the guards were about to hunt them down. He ate and ate. He did not see the hairy caterpillar twenty foot long, two foot wide and high, until its jaws began to close around his head. Then he began to run.

The dwarves found the boys asleep on the bank beside the jungle stream, flowers growing all around.

"The flowers are beautiful," sighed Julioso.

"The boys are beautiful as well," sighed Aliano and Benjio.

The boys awoke, the sound of trumpets still dancing in their minds. They were not afraid of the dwarves. They scrambled to their feet and gave each dwarf a flower.

III

At that moment Scrooey-Looey arrived. "Give me one of your bracelets Julioso," said Scrooey-Looey. Hardly knowing what he did, Julioso slipped a bracelet off his wrist and handed it to Scrooey-Looey.

The caterpillar was just behind the rabbit. He was panting loudly for he was fat and out of breath. "I only wanted to play," he complained.

"Let's play Kings and Princes," said Scrooey-Looey, "You will be King and I will bow before you, but if you are King you must wear this special bracelet round your neck."

"What is that funny thing on the front of the bracelet?" asked the caterpillar. "Your family crest," replied Scrooey-Looey. "You come from a long line of noble caterpillars: your family crest is a human skull."

"Fancy that," said the caterpillar, not noticing that all the collars and bracelets worn by the dwarves bore a human skull. "Put it round my neck. Then bow down before me."

The bracelet expanded until it fitted round the neck of the caterpillar; Scrooey-Looey lightly rubbed the skull and with a grunt the caterpillar disappeared.

At that moment a tiger arrived looking for his supper. The dwarves screamed and huddled together in a heap. Scrooey-Looey (who had grown strangely brave) said to Aliano, "Give me one of your bracelets". Hardly knowing what he did, Aliano slipped a bracelet off his wrist and handed it to Scrooey-Looey.

"Great and mighty tiger," said Scrooey-Looey. "Before you do us the honour of eating us, may I give you this bracelet: a token of our high regard for your noble person."

"For my noble person," said the tiger, much charmed by the speech. "It pleases my noble majesty to accept your gift. Then I shall do you the great honour of eating you for supper. Do I wear the bracelet on my paw?"

"No, your great and wondrous majesty," said Scrooey-Looey. "It expands like this. It would look most regal round your neck." Scrooey-Looey placed the bracelet round the neck of the tiger. The tiger looked at his reflection in the stream, as Scrooey-Looey lightly rubbed the skull and with a roar the tiger disappeared.

At that moment four cannibals arrived holding spears and shields. They were also looking for their supper. The dwarves screamed in terror as Scrooey-Looey said to them, "Give me your bracelets." Hardly knowing what they did, the dwarves slipped the bracelets off their wrists. They handed them to Scrooey-Looey.

"Great and noble warriors," said Scrooey-Looey. "Before you do us the honour of eating us, may I give you these bracelets: tokens of our high regard for your noble persons." The cannibals bowed: how nice to meet someone who knew how to behave before he was eaten.

"But what is that funny thing on the front of the bracelets?" asked the cannibals. "The skull of a missionary. Symbol of your mighty race." Much pleased, the cannibals bowed their heads as Scrooey-Looey placed a bracelet round each neck and Scrooey-Looey said: "The bracelets have a magic charm if you rub the missionary's head." Each cannibal raised an arm and rubbed the skull, and with loud cries disappeared.

"You are a marvel, Scrooey-Looey," said the boys, extremely pleased. But not the dwarves. They had just realised what they had done. Now that all six bracelets had been used they could not return the boys to Griselda. What was worse they had sent her a caterpillar twenty foot long, two foot high and wide, a tiger and four cannibals: she was not likely to be pleased. "She will hunt us down and atomise our cringing bodies," groaned the dwarves as they ran deep into the jungle.

IV

"Ah Boris, Boris," murmured Griselda tickling the skull under the chin. "I think this time the guards will get those boys." "They are extremely dim." "But with the collars they will not dare to fail. They know that I will track them down and atomise their cringing bodies." "Fear will not give them brains."

"Boris, sometimes I think you are too brainy just to be a skull," murmured Griselda gloomily. "I hate it when you're right. Those dwarves have yet to catch a thing. They are bound to fail." She rose to her feet, muttering beneath her breath: "Hate it, hate it, hate it when you're right," and kicked Boris to the top of a tree (where he yawned, stuffed cotton wool in his ears and fell asleep). Leaving her magic staff beside the cauldron she wandered through the nettles and brambles murmuring, "I wish I had some guards with brains."

As Griselda walked, deep in gloomy thoughts, out of thin air appeared the caterpillar twenty foot long, two foot wide and high. It nearly landed on her head. "Boris! Boris!" shrieked Griselda. "Come to my aid." But Boris had cotton wool in his ears and was asleep at the top of the tree as Griselda ran round the tower pursued by the caterpillar.

Then out of thin air appeared the tiger. It nearly landed on her head. "Boris!! Boris!!" screamed Griselda. But Boris was still asleep as Griselda ran and ran pursued by the caterpillar and the tiger.

Then out of thin air appeared the four cannibals holding spears and shields. They nearly landed on her head. "Boris!!! Boris!!!" yelled Griselda, running round and round the tower pursued by the caterpillar, tiger and four cannibals. Although she was ugly and scrawny, they were very keen to eat her.

Boris awoke and looking out of the sockets where once were eyes saw his mistress panting, running round and round the tower pursued by the caterpillar, the tiger and four cannibals. Boris was strangely fond of Griselda. Deciding that he must help her, he floated down from the tree and with a beam from his eye sockets lifted up the magic staff and sent it flying into Griselda's outstretched hand. Griselda turned and raised the magic staff, uttered a curse and the caterpillar (who was just about to eat her) exploded in her face, covering her with juicy innards. "Yuk!" she cried. "That was a mistake. I had better turn the tiger into stone." She raised the magic staff, uttered a curse and the tiger (who was leaping on her) turned to stone. It pinned her to the ground. "That was a mistake," groaned Griselda. "Boris! Boris! Help!!! I cannot raise the staff. The cannibals will eat me."

The cannibals got out their knives and forks. They flavoured Griselda with salt and pepper and were just about to eat her when Boris turned his sockets on the water tower. Laser beams shone from the sockets, cut through a wooden pillar and the water tower crashed to the ground, sending a great wave flowing over Griselda and the four cannibals. It swept the cannibals away but not Griselda, for she was pinned to the ground by the stone tiger.

"Boris!" spluttered Griselda, wringing wet. "You stupid skull! I nearly drowned. Get this tiger off me."

Boris floated to his mistress and sent a beam from his eye sockets which blasted the tiger to smithereens, covering Griselda with pieces of stone and choking powder. "Boris!" she gasped. "There are times you are lucky that I cannot eat you." She was raging mad. "The caterpillar, tiger and four cannibals wore around their necks the bracelets which I gave the dwarves. Boris those useless dwarves have failed. I shall go and get those boys and atomise those dwarves."

Griselda blew her hunting horn, shouted, "Tally ho! Off we go!" kicked Boris into the magic cauldron and jumped in after him. With a cry they disappeared, landing in the jungle not far from the boys and Scrooey-Looey. "I smell boys," she cried with an evil laugh. She began to run. Boris floated on her shoulder.

V

"We must hurry," cried Julius, "before Griselda gets us." They ran and ran. Griselda was only just behind. "I'm tired out," cried Benjamin, "I can't run any further." "You must," replied his brothers, taking him by the hand as they ran and ran.

Then a lion jumped out in front of them. "Help! We're going to be eaten." "No, you're not," softly roared the lion. It was the lion of icing from Alexander's birthday cake. "But you disappeared in the rain!" exclaimed the boys. "I always do, but when the sun comes out I spring to life again."

The boys and Scrooey-Looey jumped up on the lion's back. The lion ran and ran towards the Garden. As he left Griselda far behind the flowers in the shape of trumpets played a joyful tune.

The sound of trumpets filled the forest, buzzing in Griselda's ears, mocking all her evil plans. Griselda groaned, cursed and ground her teeth in pain. As the smell of boys grew fainter she bellowed in anger, "The boys are escaping but I shall get those dwarves. I feel the evil from the bands around their necks. They cannot escape. I shall atomise their cringing bodies."

"She's going to get us," moaned Julioso as the dwarves ran. "Atomise our bodies," groaned Aliano. "Blast us into nothingness," added Benjio.

The bands around their necks grew heavier. "I can hardly breathe," gasped Julioso. "Griselda must be very near," sighed Aliano. "Let's hide in the bog," suggested Benjio, who was very dim.

The dwarves jumped into the bog and hid in the mud with just their noses showing.

Griselda arrived with Boris floating on her shoulder. When she saw the three noses sticking out of the mud, she laughed an evil sneering laugh: "You cannot escape from me." She pointed her magic staff at the bog and the dwarves rose up into the air, covering Griselda with mud and slime. They landed at her feet. "Yuk!" she screamed. "You've had it. This time you've really had it. I'm going to atomise your cringing bodies." The dwarves quaked with fear. They kissed her feet. They stammered, "No, mistress," "No", "No, please." "No good!" screamed Griselda as she raised her magic staff.

At that moment Boris whispered in Griselda's ear, "Who is going to fetch the rhino sick from the shop? Who is going to get the maggots, wriggling worms and wings of bat?" Griselda went pale, paused (servants are so very hard to get) and screamed at the skull, "Boris! I hate it when you're right." She kicked the skull as far as she could and trudged off into the forest.

THE

MAGIC MAGPIE

I

The boys' father loved buying jugs. Julius said to him: "There are only two things you love: jugs and us." One day he visited an antiques fair. Behind a stall stood a horrid hag. She had a set of four jugs decorated with monsters' heads. "Good morning, sir," said the horrid hag politely. "I see you are a collector. Would you like to buy these jugs? For you a special price - £10."

It was a bargain. Quickly the boys' father got out the money. He bought the jugs and hurried home. "Boys! Boys! Come here," he cried. "Look at these fantastic jugs." As he put down the jugs in the Jug Room, the front doorbell rang and he left the room.

Julius, Alexander and Benjamin looked at the jugs. The rabbit Scrooey-Looey poked his nose inside the smallest one. The jugs began to hum and grow in size. The boys cried out in alarm as the jugs sucked them inside, and they tumbled head over heels, down and down through long winding tunnels, until with loud burps the jugs spat them out near the ruined tower in the glade deep within the forest.

Griselda was of course waiting for them. But she had made a slight mistake: the boys and Scrooey-Looey did not land at her feet; they landed beside the magic cauldron.

"Into the cauldron!" shouted Julius. "No! No! No!" screamed Griselda. "Get them, guards."

The dim daft dwarves were too slow, tripped over each other's feet and landed in a heap. The boys and Scrooey-Looey jumped in and with loud cries disappeared. They fell through the void until they landed in a forest where they walked for miles and miles until the trees began to thin.

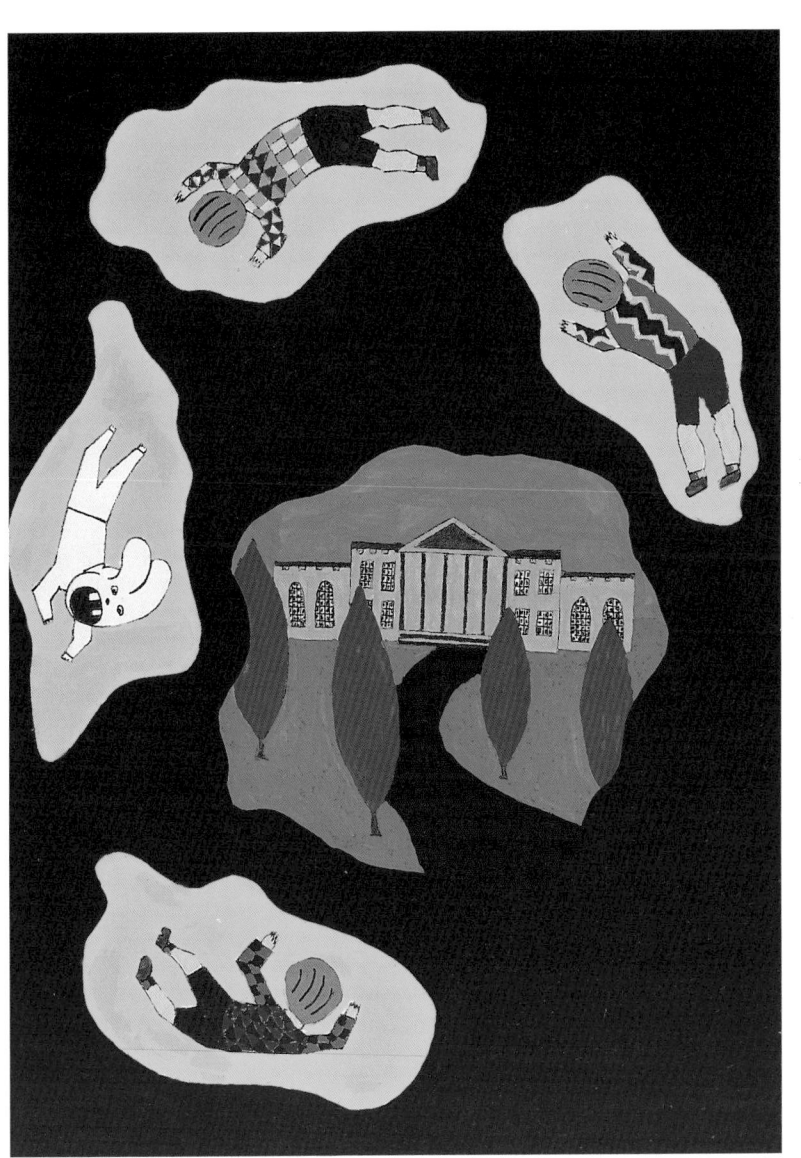

On a hillside just beyond the forest stood a palace with walls of yellow stone and gargoyles in the shape of little girls and boys. It was an evil-looking place.

"We can get supper there," said Scrooey-Looey, who was always hungry. The boys were not so sure. "They won't want boys at a palace," Julius objected. "Nor a rabbit," added Alexander.

"Rubbish!" bellowed Scrooey-Looey, running off. The brothers followed slowly through the park and up the steps to the palace. Two footmen bowed and opened the doors. "Hurry up!" squeaked Scrooey-Looey.

They walked into a hall sixty foot long and thirty foot wide and high. It had a gilded ceiling of cherubs dancing. Around the walls were paintings and sculptures: all were of boys and girls. In one corner an artist was talking about his painting to a small circle of admiring men and women. Scrooey-Looey went up and, looking at the painting, yawned and muttered, "Jolly boring." He took a crayon out of his pocket and drew pictures of rabbits on the canvas. A shriek of anguish arose from the artist and all the men and women screamed, "Go away, you boys, and you, you rabbit!"

The boys and Scrooey-Looey wandered through the palace. At the end of a corridor there was a pair of heavy doors where two footmen stood. They bowed low and opened the doors.

The boys and Scrooey-Looey entered the room where upon a throne sat a Princess, crown upon her head. "Come in, dear Alexander. How wonderful you look! Come, sit beside me on my throne. Guards, show the others to the kitchen. Put them to work." Julius, Benjamin and Scrooey-Looey were bundled off to the kitchen, Scrooey-Looey protesting, "I can't work. My beautiful white paws!"

Alexander looked in wonder at Princess Matilda. When he was seated beside her on the throne the Princess turned to her Steward, Reginald, who was standing by her side. She whispered softly: "Isn't he a beauty?" "Your highness has the very best of taste." The Princess spoke to Alexander: "Would you like a special supper just with me, without your brothers?" "Yes, I would." The Princess turned to her Steward. They exchanged glances and he left the room.

In the kitchen the cook raised a heavy ladle above Scrooey-Looey's head and shouted, "Get to work! Boys, you can dry. Rabbit, you can wash." "But my paws will get wet," protested Scrooey-Looey. "Get wet! Of course they will get wet. Hurry up or I shall put you in the stew."

The rabbit and the boys started to wash the dishes. But Benjamin was not very big and was extremely careless. After he had smashed three dishes and the cook's best pudding basin, the cook bellowed: "Stop! Stop! Stop!" "If you wish," said Scrooey-Looey, drying his paws on a dish cloth. "Not you. The little one!" shouted the cook pointing his ladle at Benjamin's head. "Go and stand in the corner."

Benjamin went and stood in the corner whilst Julius and Scrooey-Looey got back to work. The cook was decorating a cake with squiggles of icing in the shape of little boys and girls. He did not notice Benjamin creep away.

Benjamin went out of the kitchen, up stone stairs, through long corridors and then, hearing footsteps behind him, hid beneath a chair. Two men appeared carrying a wooden object. They unlocked a door close to Benjamin and carried the wooden object inside. Benjamin slipped in after them and saw a ballroom full of statues of little boys and girls. Each statue was on a wooden plinth which bore a name : "Rupert"; "Katrina"; "Cecil"; "Mary" and many others. The workmen put down the plinth in a space between two statues at the end of the room. Benjamin was not very good at reading but he realised that on that plinth there was the name "Alexander".

Silently Benjamin crept out of the ballroom, along corridors, down stairs, back to the kitchen. The cook had been so busy he had not noticed Benjamin's absence. There were two trays on the kitchen table both bearing silver dishes. The handles of one tray were decorated with crowns, the other with heads of little boys and girls. The Steward, Reginald, came in and giving the cook a tiny bottle whispered, "In the chocolate pudding would be best." Benjamin looked carefully as the cook picked up a dish on the tray which bore the heads of little boys and girls. He tipped the contents of the bottle over the chocolate pudding. Then he continued decorating the cake. Benjamin crept to Julius and Scrooey-Looey and whispered, "The Princess plans to turn Alexander into stone."

"You switch the dishes," said Scrooey-Looey, "whilst I divert the cook's attention." Scrooey-Looey took his paws out of the washing-up bowl and shouted loudly: "Pudding face!" The cook was so surprised he squirted icing up his nose. He picked up the ladle. "Were you addressing me?" "But of course. Your face is like a suet pudding."

The cook roared with anger and chased Scrooey-Looey round the table, as the rabbit shouted even louder, "Turnip head! Carrot nose!" The thing Scrooey-Looey most enjoyed (apart from food) was being rude. They ran round and round the table; then Scrooey-Looey darted out of the door into the cobbled courtyard. As he left he cried, "Arthritic slug!" The cook thundered after him.

"Quick, Julius," said Benjamin, "Help me up on to the table." Hastily he swopped the plates of chocolate pudding between the trays. As soon as he scrambled down from the table two footmen came into the kitchen. They were surprised not to find the cook and to hear the sound of shouting echoing round the courtyard. But they knew the Princess wanted her supper. Quickly they picked up the trays and took them to the smaller dining-room where the Princess was alone with Alexander. They placed the trays on the table, bowed and left.

Alexander was a fussy eater. He did not touch the soup. Of the main course he ate the roast potatoes but nothing else. The Princess began to get a little worried. "You do like chocolate pudding, do you not?" she enquired anxiously. "Oh yes," said Alexander with a smile. "Then let's get on to the pudding." They both began to eat. When the Princess ate the second spoonful she gave a choking cry and turned to stone. Alexander was surprised. At that moment Julius and Benjamin ran in. They had followed the footmen from the kitchen and had been spying through the keyhole.

"Alexander, quick, run! The Princess meant to turn you into stone but Benjamin switched the dishes." By now Scrooey-Looey had insulted not only the cook but four footmen, three maids, the artist and all his admiring men and women. Everyone was running through the palace trying to catch the rabbit. The boys hurried out of the dining room, through corridors, down stairs to the palace entrance, where they shouted, "Come on Scrooey-Looey!"

Scrooey-Looey arrived. He was hardly out of breath. "I had just begun to enjoy myself," he complained.

II

They hurried down the steps. To one side they could see Reginald rushing to get the horses and hounds. "They mean to hunt us down," cried Julius.

Off ran the boys and the rabbit, with huntsmen, horses and hounds only just behind. Suddenly a lion jumped out in front of them. "Oh help!" cried Scrooey-Looey, shaking like a jelly (for when he was not being rude he was not very brave). "It's the lion from my birthday cake," said Alexander.

"Get up on my back," softly roared the lion of icing. Once they were up, the lion ran and ran until horses, dogs and men were left far behind. "Where are you taking us?" asked the boys.

"To a royal castle. I shall tell you about it as I run. You are in the Kingdom of Alhambra. Nearly eighteen years ago, the King and Queen had an only child. Her name was Grace. The domes of the royal castle shone like golden fire. The silver keep (in which the King, Queen and Princess lived with the faithful nanny, Claire) shone like the moon. About twelve years ago Grace's mother and father disappeared. Because Grace was only five years old the Council of State appointed the King's sister as Regent to rule the kingdom until Grace reached the age of eighteen."

"What was the name of the sister?" asked Julius. "Matilda," said the lion. "The Princess who tried to turn me into stone!" said Alexander. "Will she be stone for long?" asked Benjamin. "No," replied the lion. "Her guards will get the antidote. But listen to my story.

"As soon as Matilda was appointed Regent she banished all children from the castle. 'They are common', she cried. 'They are not fit to mix with a Princess. If any child plays with the Princess, that child shall die.'

"Grace was left alone in the silver keep in the centre of the castle with her nanny, Claire. The nanny always slept in a bed beside Grace because Grace was afraid of the dark. Then Matilda gave a new command: 'It is not right that a nanny should sleep next to a Princess and a Princess breathe the same air as that breathed out by a nanny. The nanny must sleep in the dungeon.'

"At this there was some grumbling in the kingdom but many said, 'The royal line must be kept pure.' So Claire had to sleep in the dungeon deep beneath the castle keep. Claire was Grace's only friend. Matilda hoped she would soon leave but Claire was faithful. She never left the little Princess.

"All the pictures around Grace's room were of death and disaster. As it got dark the pictures glowed with ghostly light filling Grace's mind with terror. She was so afraid of the dark that she could not sleep. She spent the hours of darkness crying on her pillow until one night a magpie came to her window-sill. 'Do not cry,' said the magpie. 'I shall be your friend. But you must not tell a soul about my visits for they might try to catch me.'

"'I so much want a friend,' said the little Princess. 'No child ever comes to play with me.'

"The magpie came each night to see Grace and told her stories about Kings and Queens, Princes and Princesses, witches, ships and dragons, but every story had a sad ending. The eyes of the Princess filled with sadness. She asked the magpie (though she was only five), 'Is there nothing in the world except death and sadness?'

"'Nothing,' said the magpie. 'All the beauty of the world is like a puff of smoke. It vanishes leaving death and sadness.'

"The Princess stopped growing. The nanny tried to find a cure but could not discover what was wrong. Though Grace is now nearly eighteen, she still has the body and mind of a five-year-old, the saddest child that ever lived. She does nothing all day but sit in a chair and sew a silken banner.

"With the passing of the years the golden domes above the castle towers ceased to glow like golden fire: they became covered with green slime. The silver keep in the centre of the castle ceased to shine like the moon: it became tarnished black. The stench of evil fills the castle. Now that Grace is nearly eighteen there is to be a special meeting of the Council. Matilda will claim that because Grace still has the body and mind of a child she, Matilda, should be made Queen. Grace will lose the throne for ever."

The lion of icing stopped running. He paused for breath, for whilst he had been speaking he had run many miles. Then he continued, "The royal castle is over that hill but before I take you there I must tell you about the magpie." He was about to speak when there was a crash of thunder, a flash of lightning and rain began to pour. It soaked into the body of the lion of icing and dissolved him. As he disappeared the boys and rabbit tumbled to the ground.

III

"We must rescue the Princess," said Alexander. "But of course," replied his brothers.

Scrooey-Looey squeaked in horror: "I'll end up in the stew. It's all right for you, you're boys: you won't be eaten. I'm just a rabbit. No one cares about me." The boys took Scrooey-Looey firmly by the hand and walked over the hill. A great castle stood before them. Its towers were covered in green slime; the central keep was tarnished black. About the castle was the stench of evil and decay.

The boys and rabbit waited until it began to get dark and when the guards were not looking slipped through a gate. They found a net, which they took to help them catch the magpie (they knew she must be evil). They reached the castle keep of tarnished silver and crept up long flights of stone steps until they stood outside the bedroom of the little Princess.

Suddenly the Princess called out: "I have finished the banner. Come and look." When she saw the boys and Scrooey-Looey the Princess exclaimed in surprise, "You are not my nanny! Who are you?" "I am Julius. These are my brothers, Alexander and Benjamin. Scrooey-Looey is the rabbit." "You should not be here, but do come and see my battle banner."

The silken banner was pale blue. In the centre stood a figure, half man, half cat, holding shield and sword. "Snuggle!" exclaimed the boys. "Who is Snuggle?" asked the Princess. "Snuggle is our cat. Once, when we were chased by cannibals, he turned to hold the bridge alone. He changed into the creature sewn on your banner. Half man, half cat, he drove the cannibals back."

"That is strange," said the Princess, "for as I sewed the banner I saw Snuggle in my mind. He was riding to my aid. Where is he now?" "We don't know. Normally he comes and rescues us." "I expect he is dead," said the Princess. "All stories have a sad ending." "They don't!" cried the boys. "Let's play a game." "Getting married," commanded the Princess.

The boys groaned: why did girls like playing getting married? "I shall marry you," said the Princess pointing at Alexander. Alexander bowed politely and at the Princess's command changed into the uniform of her father when he was a cadet in the Royal Guard.

Benjamin said, "I shall be a bridesmaid." Julius and Scrooey-Looey laughed and laughed. "Benjy, not a bridesmaid. You should be a page." "No. I shall be a bridesmaid," said Benjamin. "And wear a dress. I've always wanted to be a bridesmaid. Do you have a spare dress, princess?" "You should call me 'Your Highness' but you may call me Grace. Of course I have a spare dress."

Benjamin put on the dress over his pullover and trousers and gave a twirl. "You look wonderful," cried the little Princess, clapping her hands. "Grace," said Benjamin hesitantly, "do you have a hat? I have always wanted to wear a hat covered in feathers." "I never go out," said the little Princess, "but in an old wardrobe in the dressing room there are hats which belonged to my mother."

Benjamin went into the dressing room, opened the wardrobe and chose the biggest hat he could find with great ostrich feathers which bent down over his eyes. "You look wonderful," cried the Princess. Benjamin took a bow. "No, no, you should curtsey. I shall show you how."

"Scrooey-Looey," said Benjamin, "you can be a bridesmaid too." "Not me. You must be joking," squeaked Scrooey-Looey. "Come now, Scrooey-Looey," said the Princess firmly, "put on this dress."

"I shall look such a fool," squeaked Scrooey-Looey, as he put on the dress and gave a twirl. "You look marvellous," said the Princess. "Now put on the hat." "The one with feathers," added Benjamin.

Scrooey-Looey had problems with the hat. His ears would not stay in. He put on the hat, then suddenly "flop", an ear popped out and the hat fell off. The boys and the Princess clapped their hands: "Bet the right one flops out first." "No, the left." "Here they come." Both ears flopped out together and the hat fell off. The little Princess laughed and laughed. As she laughed she began to grow. She had reached the size of seven when there was a knock upon the door. Claire, the nanny, walked in. "Good gracious!" exclaimed Claire in surprise.

"Claire, you must meet my friends: Julius, Alexander, Benjamin. Scrooey-Looey is the rabbit." "My dear, it is High Treason for a child to play with you. These boys are risking death."

"But, Claire, I am so happy. Never before have I been happy. Please bring us food and drink, then wait outside and watch. Warn us if there is danger." Claire did as she was asked, then sat on a chair outside the room and watched, her heart part joy (for she had noticed that the Princess was growing), part fear at what might happen.

"Tell me about the world," said the Princess to the boys. "I have never been outside this dismal castle. I am beginning to wonder whether what I have been told is right."

They all sat on the bed, except Scrooey-Looey who stretched out on his back taking up nearly all the room. Julius told a story about the Garden and the Gardener, Drago the dragon and Eric, his father, and their battles with Griselda. The Princess clapped her hands in joy and cried out: "The story had a happy ending! The children were not eaten. I have never heard a story with a happy ending. My nanny is forbidden on the pain of death to tell me anything. Each night after it gets dark a magpie comes, lands on the windowsill and flies into my bedroom. Then, perched on the end of my bed, she tells me stories, sad, sad stories, in which the children are always eaten. Now I know there can be a happy ending." She clapped her hands again.

The story had been long: it was dark. Claire fell asleep in the chair outside the door while the boys and Scrooey-Looey lay on the floor, their eyes growing heavy. About the room there was enchantment. The walls, which had been black, were glowing silver, shining like the moon.

Suddenly the Princess cried, "It is dark. Soon the magpie will be here. Her stories are so very sad." "If Snuggle were here," said Julius, "He would catch the magpie with a single leap. But we have brought a net. We shall do our best to catch that bird."

The Princess, Benjamin and Scrooey-Looey went into the dressing room. Julius and Alexander stretched out the net. They hid behind the sofa. It was not long before the magpie landed on the windowsill and flew to the bed, calling softly, "Grace, Grace, come and hear about a ship which travelled far, and fell off the edge of the world."

Julius and Alexander leapt, swung the net, half caught the bird but she struggled free. With a fearsome cry, she flew off, leaving some of her tail feathers caught within the net. The Princess exclaimed in surprise, "Look at the net!" The feathers had changed into a piece of purple cloth. "That is from my Aunt Matilda's dress." The doors of the room burst open. In strode Matilda, her Steward Reginald, and her guards. Matilda screamed, "Those boys and that rabbit turned me into stone. Guards! Take them to the deepest dungeon. Charge them with High Treason."

IV

Next morning the boys and Scrooey-Looey were standing in the dock. Scrooey-Looey tried to cheer them up by taking a mouth organ out of his pocket, and beginning to play a merry tune. "Silence in court! Silence in court!" bellowed the usher.

The trial was about to begin. Scrooey-Looey whispered, "I'll do the talking. I know all about courts and judges." The boys were too tactful to ask him how. The judge hurried in, sat down, removed a boot and handed it to the usher. The usher placed the boot on a wooden stand at the front of the court. "Read the charges," snapped the judge, who had got up late and missed his breakfast.

"The accused stand charged with two counts of High Treason: playing games with a Royal Princess and conspiring to marry a member of the Royal Household." "How do the accused plead?" "Say 'Not Guilty'," whispered Scrooey-Looey to the brothers. "Not Guilty," said Julius and Alexander firmly. "Not Guilty," croaked Benjamin in a little voice, for he was feeling very small.

"Did they say 'Not Guilty'?" muttered the judge. "What a waste of time. Sir Gilbert, you may proceed, but keep it short."

Sir Gilbert Carew squirmed forward on his belly and licked the judge's boot, then puffed out his chest importantly and said, "My Lord, on the night of the 15th, the accused ..." ("That's us," whispered Julius to Benjamin who was looking puzzled) "were apprehended ..." ("That means caught," whispered Julius to Benjamin) "in the bedroom of the Princess. The youngest boy and rabbit were wearing dresses."

"Dresses!" The judge was horrified. He threw down his pencil (it landed on the usher's head). "Disgusting. Absolutely disgusting. Add it to the charges. Sir Gilbert. Call your first witness." The Steward Reginald came forward and took the oath. He told how he had found the boys and Scrooey-Looey in the bedroom of the Princess. "Members of the jury," said the judge. "Do you need to retire before you return a verdict of guilty?"

Scrooey-Looey rose to his feet. "Your honour, your worship, I mean, my Lord. Might I say a word?" "Can't hear you, Mr Rabbit," snapped the judge. Scrooey-Looey squeaked a little louder, "My Lord, might I say a word?" "Can't hear you." "Might I ….," squeaked Scrooey-Looey at his loudest.

Julius poked Scrooey-Looey in the ribs. "He means he will not hear you. You forgot to lick the judge's boot." Scrooey-Looey squirmed forward on his belly, licked the judge's boot and said, "I believe it is customary to hear the defence before the verdict." "Not in my court," said the judge, "but very well, go ahead."

"My Lord," continued Scrooey-Looey, "as to the second charge of conspiring to marry. It was but a game." The judge looked intent. "So you wish to plead guilty to the first charge of playing games with the Princess. An interesting choice: you prefer to be stung to death by bees rather than to have your head chopped off."

"My Lord, how droll, how witty!" said Scrooey-Looey, rolling on the ground, helpless with laughter. He thought it was a judicial joke. "He is not joking," whispered Julius, poking Scrooey-Looey in the ribs.

The judge looked black as thunder. "Mr Rabbit, when you have quite finished, let me make myself entirely clear. The penalty for playing games with a Princess is to be stung to death by bees. The penalty for conspiring to marry is to have your head chopped off. Am I right that you admit that you are guilty of the first charge and would like to be stung to death?"

Scrooey-Looey did not know what to say. "Elect for trial by battle," whispered Julius, in a moment of sudden inspiration. Without thinking what he did, Scrooey-Looey stuttered, "I elect for trial by battle."

The judge was horrified. He threw down his pencil again. "Can he do that?" Sir Gilbert rose to his feet. "My Lord, he can. In cases of High Treason the right to trial by battle has never been removed."

"Very well but, Mr Rabbit, understand if you and those boys cannot find a champion to fight for you, it is you, Mr Rabbit, (since you made the request) who must do battle with the champion of Princess Matilda. He will chop you into little bits." Scrooey-Looey fainted. Guards picked him up and carried him off to the dungeon.

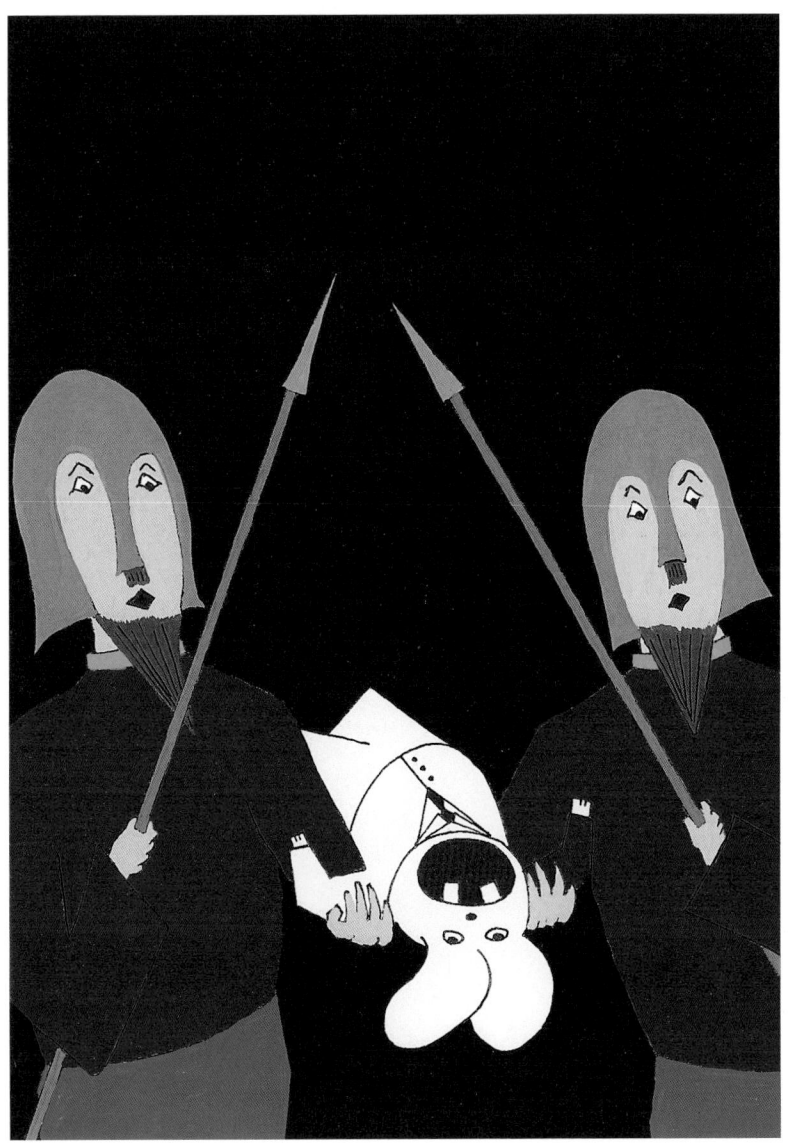

That night the boys and Scrooey-Looey lay in the dungeon. Trial by battle would take place next day. "But I am just a rabbit," moaned Scrooey-Looey. "You know I am not brave. A rabbit is very small. I cannot fight Matilda's champion. I cannot even lift a sword."

"Snuggle will come," said Julius firmly. "You saw the banner sewn by the Princess. He will not let us down." "He had better hurry," said Scrooey-Looey, moaning loudly. "I do not want to be chopped up."

No one could sleep. They lay awake on the straw, their minds full of gloomy thoughts, Scrooey-Looey moaning, "I do not want to be chopped up."

A distant bell marked each passing hour. It struck one. Their hearts were cold. Where had Snuggle got to? The bell struck two. Their hearts were heavy. Snuggle was not coming. The bell struck three. Their hearts were black. Snuggle had forgotten them. The bell struck four. Their hearts felt nothing. Snuggle had gone for ever. The bell struck five. Just as dawn was breaking, Snuggle squeezed through the bars of the dungeon window.

V

Snuggle jumped down, followed by a white cat and three kittens. "Snuggle!" shouted the boys and rabbit.

"Come now, Scrooey-Looey. Surely you did not think that I would leave you to be chopped up. You know I love a fight." "You left it jolly late," grumbled Scrooey-Looey. "We've had a wretched night." "Isn't he a hero?" purred the white cat looking at Snuggle with big, wide eyes.

"This is Fluff," said Snuggle. "And those are the brats: Achilles, Hannibal and Napoleon." "But, Snuggle, where did Fluff and the kittens come from?"

"I was on the way to rescue you when a whirlwind threw me into a deep ravine. I landed in a river, fought a crocodile with my bare paws, became a tribal god and defeated the armies of the Great Manhini." "Isn't he a hero?" said Fluff looking at Snuggle with big, wide eyes. "Then I met Fluff and had the kittens." "But it's only a few days since last we saw you." "Time was different in the ravine."

"In the Kingdom of Alhambra are you able to become half-man half-cat?" "A piece of cake," said Snuggle. "I've been practising." He turned to Julius: "I shall need armour and a horse."

"The Princess sent a message by her nanny: go to the silver keep in the centre of the castle. There you will find a suit of armour which once was worn by her father, the King of Alhambra. Lord Mountjoy will bring you a battle horse."

"Bye, Fluff! Bye, brats!" cried Snuggle. With a single leap he jumped up through the bars of the dungeon window and disappeared. "Isn't he a hero?" said Fluff looking at the dungeon window with big, wide eyes.

By ancient custom trials by battle took place in front of the silver keep. A large crowd had gathered. In the middle was a space where battle would take place. On two sides rose tiered seats for the nobility. On the other sides stood the peasants. Matilda had a special box from which she waved to the crowd. The peasants hissed back. "Peasants! Ugh! I hate them. They are so common," muttered Matilda crossly. "When will the battle start? Ah, there is my champion." A Black Rider rode up, stopped before the royal box and lowered his lance in homage. The crowd of peasants hissed.

A guard turned to Scrooey-Looey: "Come on, rabbit. Time to get ready. Where is your armour?" Scrooey-Looey was not looking brave. He was in a panic. He looked this way and that. "Where is that cat? Where is that cat?" The guard shouted, "Hurry up! I am going to enjoy seeing you chopped up." At that moment a knight in armour on a white battle horse rode out from behind the silver keep. The crowd of peasants cheered. Matilda hissed and turning to three guards whispered, "Disguise yourselves. If my champion fails, kill the boys and rabbit."

As Snuggle rode past the silver keep, Grace threw out the silken banner. He tied it to his lance. The peasants cheered and cheered. Now they knew he was Grace's champion. Matilda looked grim. "Let battle begin", she cried.

There was the crash of steel on steel as lances smashed into shields. Lances splintered and drawing swords Snuggle and the Black Rider hacked and thrust at each other until one of Matilda's guards (as Snuggle rode past) threw dust into Snuggle's eyes. The crowd of peasants hissed. Matilda cheered. As Snuggle fought for sight the Black Rider cut the leather thong which held the saddle on to Snuggle's battle horse. The horse reared up and Snuggle crashed to the ground, lying on his back stunned. The crowd of peasants hissed. Matilda cheered.

The boys and Scrooey-Looey, Fluff and the kittens all shouted, "Come on, Snuggle. Get up! Get up!" Matilda screamed in delight, "Finish him off!" The Black Rider seized another lance and rode at Snuggle, who still lay helpless on the ground. "Get up! Get up!" shouted the peasants, boys, Scrooey-Looey, Fluff and the kittens. "Get up! Get up!" "Kill! Kill! Kill!" screamed Matilda.

The Black Rider rode full tilt, lowered the lance and aimed it at Snuggle's skull. The crowd gasped in horror.   Just as the lance was about to enter Snuggle's brain he rolled to one side, grasped the lance in his bare paws, pulled the Black Rider from his horse and sat on him. "Hurrah! Hurrah!" shouted the peasants, boys, Scrooey-Looey, Fluff and the kittens. "No! No! No!" groaned Matilda.

Snuggle raised his sword, the Black Rider surrendered and Snuggle spared his life. The peasants, boys, Scrooey-Looey, Fluff and kittens cheered and cheered. Snuggle had won. The boys and Scrooey-Looey could go free.

Matilda swiftly signalled to the three guards who were standing in the crowd disguised in heavy cloaks. Swiftly they drew their swords and crept up behind the boys. Snuggle yelled a warning but could not reach the boys in time.

"We've had it," thought the boys and Scrooey-Looey, as the guards sprang towards them. But at that moment Achilles, Hannibal and Napoleon leapt at the guards, landed on their noses and dug in teeth and claws. The crowd of peasants cheered and shouted, "Get them, kittens!" Snuggle murmured proudly, "My boys! My boys!" as he ran to their aid and slew the guards with three chops of his sword.

Matilda stood at the head of her guards. She was about to shout, "Attack! Attack!" when Snuggle breathed a magic breath which showed Matilda as she really was: a princess of swirling shades of grey and black. The guards, nobles and peasants gasped in horror: it was not Matilda but the Princess of the Night! When Grace's father and mother had disappeared so had her aunt Matilda. For over twelve years the Princess of the Night had pretended to be Matilda in order to gain the throne of Alhambra.

All cried: "Death to the powers of the night!" The Princess of the Night howled in fury. Then in a puff of black smoke she disappeared.

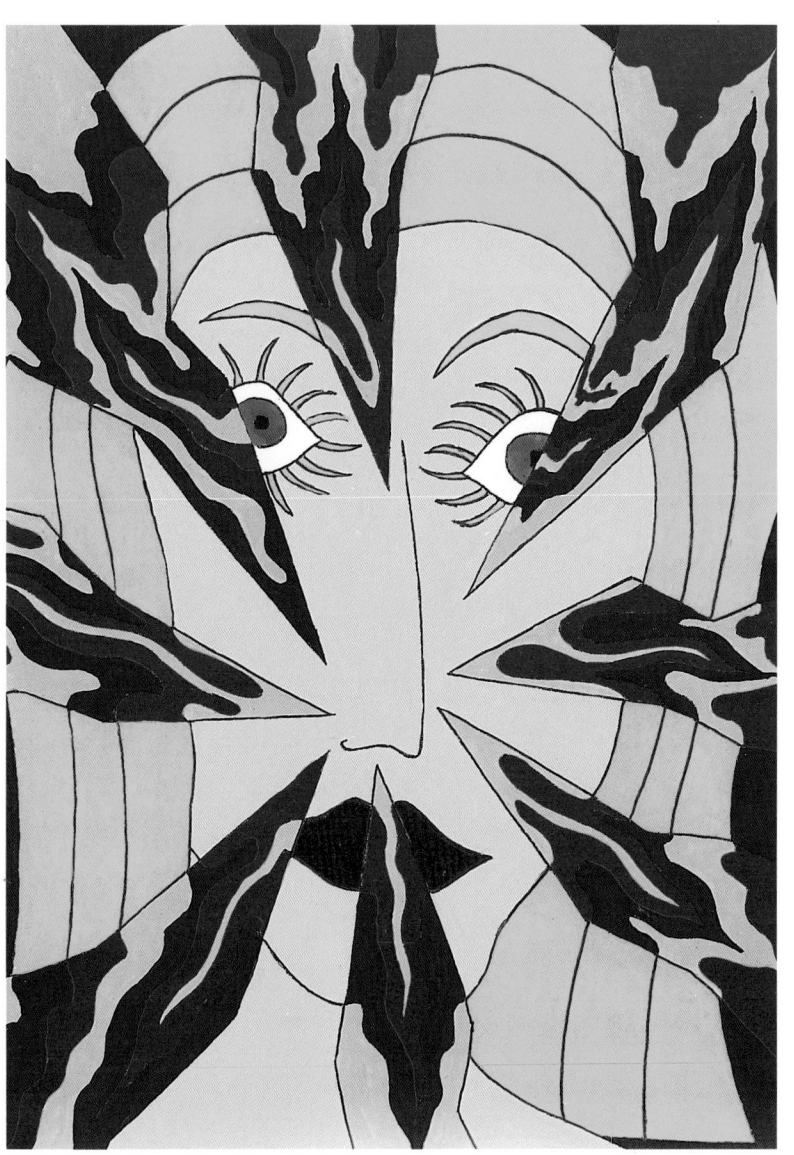

Suddenly there was the sound of trumpets. The door of the silver keep burst open and out walked the Princess, no longer a child but a young woman. The clouds parted: the sun shone brightly. The towers of gold (no longer covered in green slime) shone like golden fire. The silver keep (no longer tarnished black) shone like the moon. The crowd cheered, "Long live the Princess!"

Grace raised her arm. There was silence. Her voice rang clear: "Today I am 18. By title of my parents, the rightful King and Queen, I claim the crown of Alhambra." The crowd cheered, "Long live the Queen! Long live the Queen!"

THE
CRUEL COUNT

I

In the family vault deep below the ruined tower the dead ancestors of the witch Griselda stood in glass tanks, their flesh preserved in special fluid. Evil spirit bubbled up out of their brains, passed through tubes running from their heads, was distilled in acid and gathered in bottles of lurid green.

Above in the vaulted hall on her throne of slimy stone sat Griselda. She had just eaten well. Sadly it had not been boy or girl, but the kangaroo in dragon's blood had been unusually good: she was content. She took a swig of evil spirit.

"Boris, come here!" Griselda commanded her pet skull. Boris floated through the air and, jaw trembling, looked nervously at the magic staff in Griselda's hand.

"Boris, you lump of bone, there is no need to tremble. I do not intend to turn you into piano keys." "You don't?" "Or put you on a pole and use you as a scarecrow." "No?"

"No! No!" Griselda laughed. "I shall not even send a thunderbolt to echo in your bony skull." "You won't!" Boris began to look happier. "No! No! The meal was good. Come sit upon my lap. I shall scratch your bony head." "You will! Oh, mistress, that would be fantastic!"

Boris landed on Griselda's lap. She cradled him in her arm and scratched and tickled his bony head. The skull began to shake, his eye sockets to spin.

"Mistress ..." "Yes, Boris?" "I do like you." "You what!" "Mistress, I love you."

"Boris! You idiot!" Griselda screamed, slapping the skull on his bony cheek and rising to her feet. "You know the four-letter word beginning with L must not be used - not in Grunch Castle. It is disgusting! It is forbidden."

But the warning came too late. From the family vault deep below the tower there came the sound of breaking glass. The click, click of leather boots on stone drew near. The dim daft dwarves (Julioso, Aliano and Benjio) turned and fled. Boris floated up to a rafter and pretended to be asleep. Even Griselda trembled.

The dungeon door burst open. In marched Count Friedrich von Grunch. Dressed in military uniform, he carried a cruel cane (his magic staff); in one eye there was a monocle; his cheeks bore duelling scars. He was a terrifying sight. He had been a schoolmaster in Prussia and had invented the complete solution for the discipline of little boys: he ate them.

The Count stood to attention, clicked his heels and shouted at Griselda: "Foul cousin! Shame has been brought upon the family. Yah! The four-letter word beginning with L has been spoken. Yah! Within Grunch Castle. Yah! That is forbidden: on pain of being sent to Australia."

Each cry of "Yah!" echoed round the vaulted hall. Boris's teeth began to chatter. At the mention of Australia, Griselda turned deathly pale. The Count swished his cane through the air and pointed it at Griselda. "You are the keeper of Grunch Castle. Yah! You are responsible."

"Oh no! Not Australia!" moaned Griselda in a panic. "Anything but Australia. Boris and I were talking about hate. Boris, come here!" The skull floated down. "We were talking about hate, weren't we, Boris?" "Yes, mistress," hissed Boris loyally. The Count looked doubtful. "Yah?"

Griselda was in a sweat. Her hands trembled. "Boris only said the four-letter word beginning with L because it is so disgusting: compared with hate." "Ah, is that so?" The Count still looked doubtful. He swished his cane through the air.

"Hate! Hate! Hate!" screamed Griselda so loudly that the tower shook. She pointed her magic staff at Boris, sent a thunderflash which echoed in his bony skull and then kicked him so hard that he shot out of a window and deep into the forest where he bounced from tree to tree.

"Mein gott!" cried the Count impressed. "What a voice! What a kick! What hate! That is the way to treat a skull. I am glad that Grunch Castle is still filled with hate." "I will not be sent to Australia?" "Nein. I did not need to leave the glass tank: it was a mistake."

Griselda sighed with relief. "Foul cousin, you are welcome. Can I get you something to eat?" "Yah. I am hungry. Very hungry." The Count paused. He rubbed his belly. "A schoolboy or two would be most welcome." "Foul cousin, there is not a single boy or girl in the larder. My guards are three dim daft disgusting dwarves. They are completely useless."

"Then I must get a job as a schoolmaster. Yah! Dwarves come here!" the Count bellowed loudly. Slowly the dwarves emerged from the forest. They did not like the look of the Count. Julioso picked his nose. Aliano made a rude sound. Benjio spat in a repulsive fashion.

"Stand to attention!" shouted the Count, clicking his heels. "Stomachs in! Backs straight! Get the hands out of the pockets!" He poked the dwarves in the chest with his cane. "Never have I seen guards so dim, so daft, so disgusting. You are a disgrace. Yah!" The dwarves nodded. "Run to the shop and buy me the newspaper. Not the Daily Witch. I want to see advertisements for the job of schoolteacher." The dwarves obediently ran off.

A few days later the Count went in search of Boris. "Herr Boris!" cried the Count clicking his heels and bowing stiffly. "I have a question that I hope you can answer. Yah?" "But of course," hissed Boris. "I am applying for a post as German teacher at a school called Sevenoaks." "I have heard of it." "It is a large school. Yah?" "Quite large." "They would not miss a pupil or two. Yah?" "Possibly not," hissed Boris doubtfully.

"Good. That is good. Now tell me, skull. In the application form I am asked what punishments I favour for the discipline of boys and girls. I am worried that if I say I eat them I might not get the job. Yah?"

"Most people think that eating boys and girls is going too far," agreed Boris, thinking hard of a way to stop the Count getting the job. "You should say that you believe in capital punishment for all but the mildest offences."

"Yah? Is that so? They are more enlightened than I had thought. Thank you, Herr Boris, for your help." The Count clicked his heels, bowed stiffly and hurried off to catch the post.

The Count waited impatiently for the reply to his application. When it arrived he was not pleased. "This is beyond belief!" he cried, swishing his cane through the air. "I have not got the job. They say my ideas on discipline are too severe, that modern parents will not agree to capital punishment for their precious offspring! Mein gott!" The Count marched around the glade clicking his heels and swishing his cane. Then he had an idea. "I shall set up a school at Grunch Castle. Herr Boris! Go and get the dwarves. Yah!"

The dwarves were in the forest. They hated the look of the Count, his duelling scars, his evil swishing cane. He eyed them so hungrily: they were sure that given half a chance he would eat them. Boris found them hiding in a pile of leaves, gnashed his gnashers just behind their bottoms and brought them to the Count. "Stand to attention! Stomachs in! Backs straight!" The Count handed the dwarves a long shopping list. "Now go to the shops and buy the ingredients. Run! Run! Run!"

The dwarves ran. It took them many trips to buy all the ingredients. Each time they got back to the tower they tumbled to the ground, moaned and groaned and would not move. Then the Count looked at them through his monocle and with a hungry glint in his eye swished his cane through the air. "Stand to attention! Stomachs in! Backs straight! Run! Run! Run!" The dwarves ran. When all the ingredients had been bought the Count worked his strongest magic. With a great puff of choking smoke there arose around the tower a school, with assembly hall, classrooms, even a gym.

"Now I need the pupils", cried the Count. "I shall put an advertisement in the newspaper. But that will take time. I cannot wait." There was a hungry glint in his eye. He looked about him and saw the dwarves lying exhausted, propped up against the tower wall. "Stand to attention! Stomachs in! Backs straight! You are dim. You are daft. You are disgusting. Tomorrow you will go to school."

The dwarves began to sweat and shake. "Oh no! Not school!" "He's going to get us." "He's bound to eat us." "We hate school." "Silence!" The Count raised his cane. There was a puff of smoke and three neat piles of clothes appeared on the ground in front of the dwarves. "These are your uniforms. Tomorrow you will go to school."

II

Boris hurried to see Griselda. "Mistress!" he hissed in alarm. "The Count is forcing the dwarves to go to school. They are dim. They are daft. They are bound to get the answers wrong. The Count is going to eat them." "Ancestors!" groaned Griselda. "For hundreds of years they have stood in glass tanks in the family vault and now suddenly they start breaking out. They have no idea how hard it is to get servants. If the Count eats those dim daft dwarves, who will run to the shops?" "Mistress, perhaps I could help them," hissed Boris.

"Very well. But if you are caught by the Count, you are on your own - I know nothing about it. I am not going to be sent to Australia, not for three dim daft dwarves and a bony skull."

Next morning at an early hour a bell rang. "What is that?" cried Griselda, falling out of bed. Then she heard the Count. "Time for school! Get up you lazy dwarves! Put on your uniforms. You have five minutes," added the Count as he marched out of the shed where the dwarves slept and slammed the door behind him. The dwarves tumbled out of bed, rubbed their eyes and looked at the piles of clothes on the floor. They had never worn school uniform before.

"Four minutes!" bellowed a loud voice outside. The dwarves put on their trousers and then their pants and vests. "Three minutes!" The dwarves put on their blazers and tied their ties around their foreheads. "Two minutes!" The dwarves stuffed their socks in their pockets and put on their shoes. "What are these?" asked Benjio, pulling out the laces. "One minute!" "What about this?" asked Benjio, picking up a shirt. "Use it as a cloak," replied Aliano. The dwarves tied the shirts around their necks, put their caps on back to front and hurried out of the shed.

"Mein gott!" bellowed the Count when he saw the dwarves: he liked his food neatly dressed. "Never have I had a pupil look such a mess." The dwarves trembled. "You are dim. Yah!" The dwarves nodded. "You are daft. Yah!" The dwarves nodded. "You are disgusting. Yah!" The dwarves nodded. The Count pointed his cane at the dwarves' heads and muttered a magic word. There was a blinding flash and the dwarves found that they were neatly dressed. "That is better," cried the Count. "Now stand to attention! Stomachs in! Backs straight! Into the classroom. Run! Run! Run!"

"What about breakfast?" murmured Julioso, picking his nose. "Breakfast!" snapped the Count, a hungry glint in his eye. "First the spelling tests and the maths. Then the breakfast. Ha! Ha! Ha!"

The dwarves ran into the classroom and sat down at the desks. The Count strode in after them, swishing his cane through the air. "First I shall explain the rules. In this school discipline is very strict. Ha! Ha! Ha!" He licked his lips. "I shall ask each of you five questions. If you get more than two wrong, then for each wrong answer I shall nibble off a finger or toe."

The dwarves were in a panic. Their teeth began to chatter. "We're fond of our fingers." "And our toes." "We'll miss them." "No talking in class. I shall start with you." He pointed at Julioso with his cane. "How do you spell 'knee'?" Julioso scratched his bottom, then said slowly, "N-E-E." "Wrong. How do you spell 'wrong'?" Julioso scratched his head, then said in a trembling voice, "R-O-N-G." "Wrong." The Count rubbed his hands.

Julioso was in a dreadful state. He wriggled his fingers; he wriggled his toes. "Goodbye, fingers! Goodbye, toes!" he murmured to himself. But at that moment Boris appeared, with pen and paper between his teeth. The Count did not see him as he floated near the ground between the desks.

"How do you spell 'psalm'?" snapped the Count. Quickly Boris wrote it down in large letters. "P-S-A-L-M," said Julioso, looking out of the corner of his eye at the paper on the ground. "Mein gott!" The Count ground his teeth in disbelief. "How do you spell 'hippopotamus'?" Quickly Boris wrote it down. "H-I-P-P-O-P-O-T-A-M-U-S," said Julioso. "Mein gott! You are not so dim as I had thought. But I shall get you yet. How do you spell 'encyclopaedia'?" Boris wrote it down. "E-N-C-Y-C-L-O-P-A-E-D-I-A."

Julioso wriggled his fingers and toes: he was very glad to keep them. But not the Count. He nearly choked with disappointment. "My breakfast! Mein gott! I cannot believe it. Very well, we shall try you." He pointed his cane at Aliano's head. Aliano began to sweat. The Count was standing so close to the desks that Boris (who was still underneath Julioso's desk) did not dare move closer to Aliano.

"We shall do multiplication. Yah?" Aliano looked completely blank. "Tables." "Oh." "What are 2 x 4?" Aliano guessed wildly: "6." "Wrong." The Count rubbed his hands and licked his lips. "What are 3 x 5?" Aliano had no idea. "Well! We do not have all day. What is the answer?" Aliano looked at the floor but Boris was still under Julioso's desk. He guessed wildly: "24."

"Wrong!" The Count cried triumphantly, swishing his cane through the air. Aliano was in a dreadful state. He wriggled his fingers, wriggled his toes. "Goodbye fingers! Goodbye toes!" he murmured to himself. But at that moment the Count made a mistake. In his excitement he turned his back on the dwarves. Quickly Boris floated underneath Aliano's desk.

"Got him! Got him! Got him!" murmured the Count to himself. "Nibbling time will soon be here. But I must take no chances." He turned to Aliano. "What is 7 x 9?" Quickly Boris wrote it down. "63," said Aliano. "Mein gott!" cried the Count. "He has got it right. I must try another question. What is 8 x 11?" Quickly Boris wrote it down. "88," said Aliano without hesitation.

The Count ground his teeth in disbelief. "If I am not careful, I shall lose my breakfast. What is 9 x 33? Quick, dwarf, in your head. Haven't you done your 33 times table yet?" He rubbed his hands. "This time I have got him," he murmured to himself. Fortunately Boris was the latest model of skull. He had a calculator built into his head. Quickly he wrote the answer down. "297," Aliano said.

The Count could not believe it. His monocle fell out of his eye and he nearly choked. "You must be cheating!" He pointed his cane at Aliano's head. "Stand up, dwarf," he cried. Reluctantly, Aliano got to his feet. The Count strode towards him. He looked underneath the desk. Boris tried to hide but was too slow. "Mein gott!" bellowed the Count. "The skull! I shall blast him into nothingness."

By now Boris was moving very fast. He whizzed between the desks. "Stand still, skull! Take your punishment like a man!" bellowed the Count as he swung his cane and a desk was blasted into nothingness. Round and round went Boris, zooming between the desks, zooming underneath the desks, zooming up and down, round and round, as the Count blasted desks, chairs and blackboard, but failed to get the skull.

Griselda heard the shouting and came running. When she saw the dwarves cowering in a corner of the room, she sent them to the shop to get the shopping, then bellowed at the Count: "How dare you try to blast my skull! He's my property. Leave him alone." The Count had never heard a woman with such a loud voice. "Mein gott!" he murmured to himself, breaking into a sweat. Then he protested: "Herr Boris helped those dwarves to cheat." "But he's my property," cried Griselda proudly. "If he is to be blasted, it shall be done by me."

"Very well, I shall leave the skull. But tomorrow the dwarves must come to school. Herr Boris will not save them then." The Count swished the cane through the air and marched off, belly empty, extremely angry.

Boris floated to Griselda. "Mistress, thank you for saving me. Perhaps you l-o-v-e me after all." "Shut up, Boris!" screamed Griselda. "Don't be so wet and soppy. We're in enough trouble without you saying the four-letter word beginning with L. Whoever l-o-v-e-d a skull! You must be mad. Next time you try to help the dwarves make sure you do not get caught." So saying, Griselda kicked Boris out of the window. He landed deep in the forest and bounced from tree to tree as Griselda stalked off in a sulk. "The Count is bound to eat those dwarves. Then who will go to the shops to buy my tea?"

III

That night the dwarves were not happy. As they lay in their beds in the shed propped up against the ruined tower, they could not sleep. They moaned softly, "The Count will get us." "He'll eat us for breakfast." "Goodbye fingers!" "Goodbye toes!" In the middle of the night Julioso had an idea. "Let's run away," he said. The dwarves were a little surprised they had not thought of this before. "What a good idea!" cried Aliano. "Why didn't I think of that?" murmured Benjio, scratching his head.

Quickly they got out their rucksacks and put in tins of baked beans and peaches, but forgot to take a can opener. They put in a paraffin stove, but forgot to take a box of matches. They forgot the map and compass (not that they knew how to use them) and filled up the rucksacks with old newspapers, not having anything else to take. With beating hearts they crept out of the shed. The door creaked: the dwarves froze. An owl hooted: the dwarves hugged each other in terror. Slowly they made their way through the glade. Snakes slithered; spiders scurried out of their way; bats flitted across the night sky. With every step the dwarves' hearts beat louder. They were going to be caught. The Count would awake. He would eat them for his breakfast. But no one stirred in the tower. Boris (in the top of a tree) opened one eye but quickly pretended to be asleep. When the dwarves reached the trees at the edge of the glade, they ran and ran. They were free.

However, progress was slow in the dark. They bumped into trees and became entangled in bramble bushes. It was getting light as they approached a clearing. "Great!" "We've reached the end of the forest." "We'll get on faster now."

Out they rushed into the clearing. It was the glade deep within the forest. The school and ruined tower stood before them and a loud voice bellowed: "Come here, dwarves. Where do you think you're going?" The Count swished his cane through the air. "What! Not in your uniforms? It is nearly time for school. Stomachs in. Backs straight. Run, run, run."

The dwarves were about to go into the shed to change for school when Benjio had an idea. He did not know where it came from. His mind was a total blank when suddenly he said, "Let's jump into the magic cauldron." "Nein! Nein! Nein!" bellowed the Count, but he was too slow. Before he could stop the dwarves, they dived into the magic cauldron and with loud cries disappeared.

The dwarves fell into the Land of Nothingness, limbs all muddled up in nothingness. In that land nothing had substance: all was mist in different shades of swirling grey. The dwarves struggled to their feet, and sighed, "We've turned into nothingness." They floated, hardly able to distinguish between different shades of grey, where a foot or arm ended and the ground or sky began. "I don't like it," murmured Benjio, as he floated into a tree of solid mist and his body swirled around it. "This is odd," cried Julioso, as he tripped and his fist swirled through Aliano's head.

The dwarves had not travelled far when out of the mist there rode a princess of swirling shades of black and grey upon a horse of nothingness. Behind her ran two yapping dogs of swirling mist. "Brave sirs, welcome to my kingdom. I can see by your noble looks that you are mighty warriors. Come and join me in my palace." The dwarves looked around. "Where are the mighty warriors?" "Is she talking to us?" "But of course. Are you not brave and noble warriors fit to serve a princess?"

"Not us - we're cowards." "Yellow through and through." "You must be thinking of someone else." The princess cursed and rode off into the mist.

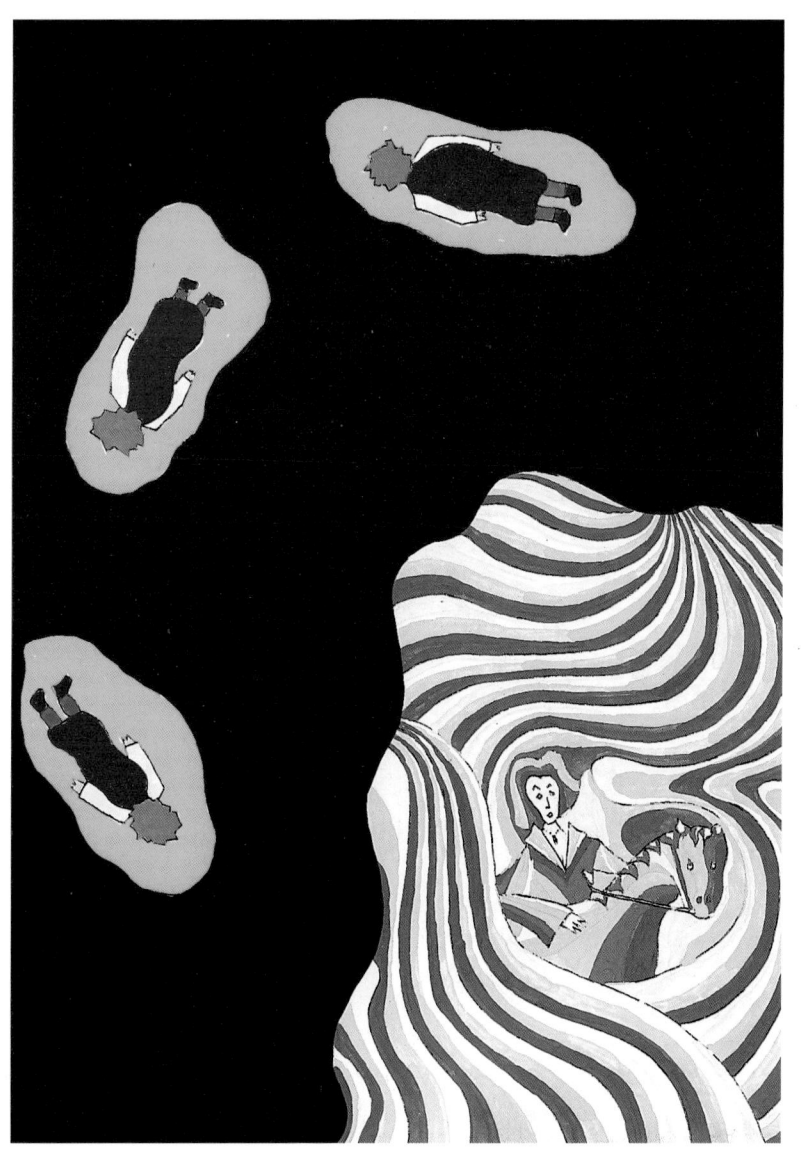

The dwarves had not travelled much further when out of the mist there emerged a black sedan chair of swirling mist carried by four surly servants dressed in black. A grey hand drew back the curtain and the princess said, "Fair sirs, welcome to my kingdom. I can see by your looks that you are young persons of grace and beauty. Come and join me in my palace."

The dwarves looked blank. "Grace and beauty!" "She must be joking." "Surely not us." "But, yes. Are you not young persons of grace and beauty fit to serve a princess?" "Not us - we're dwarves." "We're ugly." "Always have been, always will be." The princess cursed. She shouted at her servants, who carried the sedan chair off into the mist.

The dwarves had not travelled much further when the princess emerged once more out of the mist. She was on foot. She did not look happy. Setting her face in a ghastly smile, she cried, "Young sirs, I can tell by your lofty brows that you are dwarves of intelligence and wit. Come and grace my palace."

The dwarves just laughed. "Intelligence!" "Wit!" "We're dim." "We're daft." "We're thick." The princess cursed and disappeared. As she did so, the mist began to change from black to deep grey-blue. The sun rose above a distant hill, drawing the mist towards it and as blackness and greyness faded the dwarves became more solid. "I'm me, I'm me again," cried Julioso excitedly. "Let's test it." So saying he punched Aliano on the jaw. Aliano fell to the ground and rubbed his jaw. "Great! Great! Great! I'm no longer mist."

The dwarves were on a hillside. Looking down they could see trees emerging from the mist, blackness changing to fields of green, brown and gold. "It's so beautiful, we should not be here." "It's too beautiful for us." "We're too dim and daft for anything so lovely." Then they heard a purring sound and saw a cat stretched out on the grass. The cat rolled over. "He wants to be stroked." "He looks like Snuggle." "But this cat is not fierce, he's friendly." So saying Benjio bent down and stroked the cat's tummy. The cat purred.

The dwarves were so intent they did not hear the Count approach. Suddenly he bellowed: "Stand up straight! Stomachs in! Surely you did not think that you could escape! It's time for school - and then my breakfast!" The Count licked his lips and raised his cane. There was a flash and a net sprang round the dwarves. As they were pulled deep into the void, the cat crept away.

IV

The dwarves landed in a heap in the glade in front of the Count. "You are ugly. Yah! You are disgusting. Yah!" He raised his cane. There was a flash and the dwarves stood neatly in a line, dressed in school uniform. "Into the classroom. Run. Run. Run."

When they reached the classroom they saw a golden-haired boy sitting in the front row. He rose to his feet. "Good morning, sir," he said, smiling sweetly. "Who are you?" barked the Count. "Where did you come from?" "I'm the new boy, sir." "Where are your parents?" "I'm an orphan, sir." "You have no one who would miss you?" "No one, sir."

The Count licked his lips. "Good. Sit down. Discipline here is very strict. I am about to start a maths test. Then it will be breakfast." The Count strode to the blackboard. He was writing out a sum when a paper dart sailed through the air and hit him on the ear.

"Mein gott!" bellowed the Count. He turned and stared at the dwarves, who were shaking with fear. "Which dwarf threw that?" "Not us." "We didn't do it." "No, please."

The Count turned to the new boy. "Did you throw the dart?" The new boy smiled sweetly, "Oh, yes, sir. Isn't it a beauty!" "Mein gott! I said discipline is strict. Strict. Strict. Strict." The Count suddenly thought of something: he had forgotten his false teeth. "Stand there. I shall be back directly."

The dwarves were in a state of terror, legs and arms shaking, teeth chattering, heads nodding from side to side, but the new boy stood there wholly unconcerned. Hands in pockets he whistled softly, then picked up a wastepaper basket. He placed it upside down on the top of the door into the classroom and put an upturned chair just inside the door.

False teeth gnashing, the Count strode through the door. The wastepaper basket landed on his head. "Mein gott! Who turned out the light?" The Count fell over the upturned chair, landed with a crash amidst the desks, struggled to his feet, tore the wastepaper basket off his head and barked, "Who did that?" "Not us!" "Not us!" "Not us, sir!" stammered the dwarves.

"Was it you?" bellowed the Count, pointing his cane at the new boy. "Who, me, sir? Oh, yes, sir." "It was! In this school discipline is very strict." The Count licked his lips. He put a hand into his coat pocket for his knife and fork. He was just about to grasp the boy by the neck, when the boy darted underneath the Count's outstretched arm and dashed to the door.

"Stand still and be eaten like a man!" shouted the Count. "Yah, boo, sucks!" cried the boy, sticking out his tongue and running through the doorway. "Mein gott! Come back!" bellowed the Count as, knife and fork in hand, he rushed after the boy and out into the glade.

The boy disappeared behind a bush and as the Count strode across the glade, pulled taut a rope with one end tied to a tree. The Count tripped, did a somersault, landed in the magic cauldron and with a loud cry disappeared. The new boy ran off into the forest and changed into a cat. As the Count disappeared his magic was destroyed: the dwarves became their normal scruffy selves and the school vanished.

The Count tumbled down and down through the void and landed in the Kingdom of the Deep. Young sharks were just coming out of school. They had been having a lesson about the human body, where to find the juicy bits. When they saw the Count they blew bubbles in delight: they could hardly believe their luck.

"Bagsy the nobbly bit on top!" "That's the head, dumbo. It contains hardly any meat." "I want a leg." "That's not fair. You always get a leg." "Save a bit for me." That was the end of the Count.

"Thank goodness for that!" cried Griselda. "I am fed up with ancestors. Boris, come here." "Yes, mistress." "If you ever say that four-letter word again I'll put you on a pole and use you as a scarecrow." "Yes, mistress." "Or change you into piano keys." "Mistress, are you sure you don't like me?" "Boris! Shut up!"